The Great Goat Gaffe

Don't miss a single

Nancy Drew Clue Book:

Nancy Drew

* CLUE BOOK *

#15

The Great Goat Gaffe

BY CAROLYN KEENE * ILLUSTRATED BY PETER FRANCIS

Aladdin

NEW YORK   LONDON   TORONTO   SYDNEY   NEW DELHI

ALADDIN

An imprint of Simon & Schuster Children's Publishing Division
1230 Avenue of the Americas, New York, New York 10020
First Aladdin paperback edition March 2021
Text copyright © 2021 by Simon & Schuster, Inc.
Illustrations copyright © 2021 by Peter Francis
Also available in an Aladdin hardcover edition.
NANCY DREW, NANCY DREW CLUE BOOK,
and colophons are registered trademarks of Simon & Schuster, Inc.
All rights reserved, including the right of reproduction in whole or in part in any form.
ALADDIN and related logo are registered trademarks of Simon & Schuster, Inc.
For information about special discounts for bulk purchases, please contact Simon & Schuster
Special Sales at 1-866-506-1949 or business@simonandschuster.com.
The Simon & Schuster Speakers Bureau can bring authors to your live event.
For more information or to book an event contact the Simon & Schuster Speakers Bureau
at 1-866-248-3049 or visit our website at www.simonspeakers.com.
Series designed by Karina Granda
Book designed by Heather Palisi
The illustrations for this book were rendered digitally.
The text of this book was set in Adobe Garamond Pro.
Manufactured in the United States of America 0121 OFF
2 4 6 8 10 9 7 5 3 1
Library of Congress Cataloging-in-Publication Data
Names: Keene, Carolyn, author. | Francis, Peter, illustrator.
Title: The great goat gaffe / by Carolyn Keene ; illustrated by Peter Francis.
Description: First Aladdin hardcover/paperback edition. | New York: Aladdin Books, 2021. |
Series: Nancy Drew clue book ; [#15] | Audience: Ages 6 to 9. | Audience: Grades 2–3. |
Summary: When a badly-behaved goat that is gaining Internet fame ruins a "Kids with Kids"
yoga class, eight-year-old Nancy Drew and her friends
investigate how it got to Sweet Creams Farm.
Identifiers: LCCN 2019027420 (print) | LCCN 2019027421 (eBook) |
ISBN 9781534450271 (paperback) | ISBN 9781534450288 (hardcover) |
ISBN 9781534450295 (eBook)
Subjects: CYAC: Goats—Fiction. | Farm life—Fiction. | Yoga—Fiction. |
Mystery and detective stories.
Classification: LCC PZ7.K23 Gre 2021 (print) | LCC PZ7.K23 (eBook) | DDC [Fic]—dc23
LC record available at https://lccn.loc.gov/2019027420
LC eBook record available at https://lccn.loc.gov/2019027421

* CONTENTS *

Chapter

MEET AND BLEAT

"What could be better than spring break?" George Fayne asked.

"Spring break and spring clothes?" Bess Marvin said.

Eight-year-old Nancy Drew smiled at her two best friends. "Spring break and feeding goats here at Sweet Creams Farm!" she declared.

It was a sunny Tuesday in early spring. Nancy, Bess, and George were often busy solving mysteries as the Clue Crew. This day, they were busy volunteering at Sweet Creams Farm.

To the girls, Sweet Creams was the best farm ever. Not only did it sell goat cheese, yogurt, and ice cream, but it had its own petting zoo filled with tiny Pygmy goats!

"Hey, you guys!" George chuckled as three goats tried to drink out of the bottle she clutched. "One per customer!"

But the goats at Sweet Creams weren't only for feeding or for petting. They were part of a cool new class at Sweet Creams—goat yoga!

"Feeding tiny goats is super fun," Nancy said as they carefully placed empty bottles in a wooden crate, "but I wish we could join a real live goat yoga class."

"Yoga is supposed to be so relaxing!" Bess added.

"What's relaxing about twisting yourself into a pretzel while goats climb all over you?" George asked. "I'd rather play soccer."

The three friends left the pen to make room for the goat yoga class. People chatted excitedly as they laid their mats on the soft grassy ground. Some curious goats were already wandering around the mats, bleating softly.

Nancy, Bess, and George watched through the fence as the yoga instructor, Nina Pickles, began the class. Besides teaching yoga, Nina had her own store where she sold activewear and workout clothes.

"Be one with the goats as we enter the low lunge," Nina told the class. "And be sure to check out the low sale prices at Nina Pickles Activewear. This week only!"

Nancy, Bess, and George traded smiles. Nina was always looking for ways to spread the word about her store.

"Let's lie on our stomachs for the cobra pose," Nina instructed. "Cobra, as in the new snakeskin-design leggings just in at my store!"

"Baaaaa!" one of the tiny goats bleated as he scampered onto a posing man's back.

"Pygmy goats are as small as puppies," Bess pointed out. "It's hard to tell which ones are the babies."

"You mean *kids*," George said. "We learned here on the farm that baby goats are called kids, remember?"

Kids! The word made Nancy's eyes light up.

"Bess, George, the most awesome idea just popped into my head! What if Sweet Creams Farm had a goat yoga class for kids?"

"You mean human kids, like us?" Bess asked.

"Yes," Nancy said. "The class can be called . . . Kids with Kids!"

"Cool!" Bess exclaimed.

"Cool for other kids," George said as they watched a goat crawl onto a woman's shoulder. "Like I said, I'll stick to soccer."

"I bet you'll like goat yoga too, George." Nancy giggled. "Let's find Sophie and see what she thinks."

Sophie Sweet was the energetic woman who ran Sweet Creams Farm. Nancy, Bess, and George found her at the farm stand unpacking bottles of goat milk smoothies.

After hearing Nancy's idea, she smiled. "A

goat yoga class for kids would be great for Sweet Creams Farm," she said. "And for *Wake Up, River Heights*!"

"*Wake Up, River Heights*?" Nancy repeated. "You mean the TV show that's on super early in the morning?"

"Correct!" Sophie said. "A crew is coming to the farm tomorrow morning to film our goat yoga class." Sophie gave an excited little hop. "With spring break this week, a goat yoga class just for kids would be perfect!"

"Oooh!" a voice exclaimed. "Perfect for me, too!"

The girls turned to see Nina Pickles, a towel draped over one shoulder.

"Why aren't you with your class, Nina?" Sophie asked.

"I left them in the deep relaxation pose," Nina explained, "but who can relax with news about a goat yoga class for kids?"

Nancy couldn't believe her ears. "You like my idea too, Ms. Pickles?" she asked.

"Sure I do!" Nina said. "I'm unveiling my new line of kids activewear this week. What better time to introduce it than on TV?"

"Oh," Sophie said, hesitating. "I'm afraid that's not a good idea, Nina."

"Why not?" Nina asked, surprised.

"*Wake Up, River Heights* wants to cover goat yoga," Sophie explained, "not fashion."

Nina gasped. "Everything is about fashion, Sophie!" She closed her eyes and took deep breaths through her nose before adding, "I think you'd better find another yoga instructor for tomorrow."

The girls watched as Nina huffed back to the goat yoga pen and her class.

"Will Nina be okay, Sophie?" Nancy asked. "She seemed very upset."

"She'll get over it, I'm sure," Sophie said. "In the meantime, I have an important job for you girls."

"A job?" Bess gulped. "You don't want us to clean the goat pen, do you?"

"No, Bess." Sophie chuckled. "I need you to find kids for our goat yoga class tomorrow. They need to be here at seven thirty sharp."

"No problem, Sophie," Nancy said quickly. "We have lots of friends and classmates to invite."

"Getting them to be on TV will be easy," George added.

"Easier than cleaning the goat pen!" Bess said, clearly relieved.

"Good! I'll get some permission slips to give to your friends," Sophie said. "Tell them to bring their slip signed by a parent tomorrow."

Sophie went to her office for the permission slips.

The girls couldn't wait to find kids for the goat yoga class!

"I am soooo excited!" Bess said. Then, "What are we going to wear to the goat yoga class?"

"Goat footprints," George joked.

Nancy smiled and said, "As soon as we get the permission slips, let's go to Main Street. We'll find lots of kids there."

Nancy, Bess, and George all had the same rules. They could walk anywhere, as long as it was under five blocks—and as long as they were together. Together was more fun anyway.

When the girls reached Main Street, they found lots of kids they knew. But most of the kids knew nothing about yoga. . . .

"I like frozen yoga," Peter Patino said, pointing to the nearby fro-yo shop. "Will they have chocolate or strawberry?"

Some kids had heard about yoga, but not goat yoga. When the girls invited Kendra Jackson, she asked, "Are the goats gentle?"

George nodded. "You won't know there's a goat on your back," she explained, "until you smell the hay on its breath!"

"Ew," Kendra said, wrinkling her nose.

When the girls asked Henderson Murphy, he shook his head. "I watch *Danger Dog* at that time every morning," he said. "Tomorrow is the flea circus episode."

"You'd rather watch TV than be on TV?" George groaned. "Whatever!"

The girls left Henderson and walked up Main Street. When they ran out of kids to invite, they turned onto Magnolia Street.

"I don't blame Henderson for wanting to see *Danger Dog* tomorrow," Bess said. "The flea circus episode rocks."

"What if *everybody* wants to watch *Danger Dog* tomorrow morning?" George asked, imagining the worst. "What if no one shows up?"

Nancy wasn't too worried. "Some kids said yes, some said no, and a few said maybe," she stated. "Let's hope for the best."

The three friends were about to make their way home when—"*Baaaaa! Baaaaa! Baaaaa Baaaaa!*"

Nancy, Bess, and George froze. Had they just heard what they thought they'd heard?

"Was that . . . a goat?" Nancy asked.

"For sure," George said, looking around.

"After being at the farm all day, I know a goat when I hear one."

"Except we're not on the farm," Bess said. "We're on Magnolia Street."

The girls followed the sound to the middle of the block. George pointed to a green house with white shutters. "It's coming from the Dishers' house," she said.

Eight-year-old Leslie Disher was in the girls' class at school. Leslie loved writing in her journal. She also worshipped teen singing idol Brad Sylvester. Nancy, Bess, and George didn't know Leslie's twin brother, Wesley, as well. He was in the other third-grade class.

"Baaaaaaa!"

The bleating grew louder as Nancy, Bess, and George followed it to the backyard. A big trampoline was set up there. But it wasn't Leslie or Wesley jumping up and down on it. It was a tiny white-and-brown Pygmy goat!

"Baaaa! Baaaa!" the goat bleated as it bounced sky-high. The girls couldn't believe their eyes as

they watched the goat perform awesome front flips and backflips and midair spins!

"That's a goat all right," Nancy said.

"Not just any goat, Nancy!" George said with a grin. "That's *Pogo*!"

Chapter

GOAT FOR IT!

"Pogo?" Bess repeated.

"How do you know his name, George?" Nancy asked.

"Here's how," George said, reaching for a phone in her jacket pocket. "Pogo is a rising YouView star. He already has a ton of likes!"

Bess gasped as they watched Pogo's YouView video. "I like him too. Look at him go!"

With her fingers, George enlarged the video. "Not only is Pogo a trampoline star," she pointed out, "he's got a brown star-shaped mark on his side. How random is that?"

Nancy smiled as she looked from the video to the real goat on the trampoline. "I heard about Pogo," she said, "but I didn't know he lived right here in River Heights."

"That's because *I* live in River Heights," a voice piped up, "and Pogo is my pet!"

The girls turned to see Wesley Disher walking over holding a book in his hand. As he got closer, Nancy could read the title: *Raising Your Pet Goat*.

"This book says what to feed a goat, where to keep it, and how to play with it too," Wesley said as he flipped through the pages. "It says nothing about goats on trampolines though!"

"Maybe because Pogo is a special goat, Wesley," Nancy said.

Bess turned to George. "Make your own video, George. Go ahead!"

But the minute George lifted her phone camera—

"Stop!" someone shouted. "Don't even think about it."

Turning again, the girls saw another boy from school, third-grader Quincy Taylor, walking quickly toward them shaking his head.

"No videos, please," Quincy told George. "And if you want to interview Wesley about Pogo, you have to go through me first."

"Since when?" George asked.

"Since I became Pogo's manager," Quincy said proudly.

Nancy wasn't surprised that Quincy had a new job. He was always jumping into some new project or club. "Did you put Pogo's video up on YouView, Quincy?" she asked.

"Sure, and that's just the beginning," he said. "Once I get word out about Pogo, there'll be Pogo toys, Pogo books—maybe even a Pogo TV show."

Pogo hopped off the trampoline, landing on all fours. He gave another bleat before padding over to the girls.

"Speaking of TV," Nancy said, "you're both

invited to a special goat yoga class at Sweet Creams Farm tomorrow morning."

"Very early!" George added. "The class will be shown on *Wake Up, River Heights* at seven thirty."

"Goat yoga?" Wesley asked.

"There's a pen at Sweet Creams Farm with goats just like Pogo," Bess explained. "They really love crawling and jumping on posing people."

Wesley thought about it, then shook his head. "No, thanks," he said. "Seven thirty is way too early during spring break."

"Not for Pogo," Quincy declared. "That show is just what he needs for his TV debut!"

Nancy glanced at Bess and George. She knew they were thinking the same thing she was. Sweet Creams already had plenty of goats for the goat yoga class.

"Thanks, Quincy," Nancy said. "We're pretty sure Sophie Sweet is all set with goats for tomorrow morning."

"Besides," George said, "Pogo should stick to trampolines, not yoga mats."

"Okay, okay." Quincy sighed as he reached into his pocket. "If Pogo can't be on the show, can you at least wear these to spread the love?"

Quincy pulled out three purple bangle bracelets. Each sturdy paper bracelet had Pogo's name printed on it. He handed one each to Nancy, Bess, and George. Wesley was already wearing a Pogo bracelet on his wrist.

"You just wait," Quincy declared. "Soon Pogo will have left his mark on everyone!"

Bess pointed to Pogo nibbling on Wesley's purple bracelet. "You mean *teeth marks*!" She giggled.

The girls said goodbye to Wesley, Quincy, and even to Pogo. They rounded the house and made their way back to the sidewalk. Standing at a blue recycle bin was Wesley's twin sister, Leslie.

Leslie muttered to herself as she shoved something deep into the bin. "Dumb goat . . . dumb goat . . . dumb goat!"

"Hi, Leslie," Nancy said.

"That dumb goat you were mumbling

about . . . ," George said. "You can't mean Pogo."

"Oh, yes I can!" Leslie shouted. "Look what that shrub-breath did to this. Look!"

Leslie reached deep into the bin and pulled out a large poster. It was shredded from top to bottom like linguine!

"This *was* my latest poster of Brad Sylvester. I

left it in the backyard after showing my friends, and Pogo got to it!"

Leslie tossed the damaged poster back into the can. "It even smelled like Brad's favorite candy: Watermelon Wowsies."

"Now it smells like garbage," Bess said, pinching her nose.

"Thanks to Pogo," Leslie snapped. "So far he's chewed up my rain boots, my favorite sunglasses, and just about all of my Brad Sylvester mementos."

"I guess Pogo isn't a Brad Sylvester fan," joked George. "Why did your family get a goat in the first place?"

"I wanted a cute little kitten or puppy, but Wesley wanted a goat," Leslie explained. "He's two minutes older, so guess who won." Slamming down the lid, Leslie muttered, "I wish Pogo would just get lost."

"That was harsh," Nancy whispered as Leslie walked toward her house. "Leslie doesn't seem to like Pogo much."

"But I saw a purple Pogo bracelet around

Leslie's wrist," George said. "Why would she wear one if she doesn't like Pogo?"

"Because she likes the color purple?" Bess guessed.

The girls forgot about Pogo as they headed up Magnolia Street. By then even George was getting used to the idea of a goat yoga class.

"Why don't we practice some yoga poses?" Bess suggested, stretching her arms high above her head. "I know the cat, the cow, the cobra, the downward-facing dog—"

"There's only one yoga pose I know," George cut in, twisting her arms this way and that. "The corkscrew pasta!"

Very early the next morning, Hannah drove Nancy, Bess, and George to Sweet Creams

Farm. As she pulled into the parking lot, she said, "The farm's market is open early. Why don't I do some shopping while you girls do goat yoga?"

Hannah Gruen was the Drews' housekeeper, but she was more like a mother to Nancy. Since Nancy was three, Hannah had made sure she brushed her teeth twice a day, ate her vegetables, got up in time for school—and got lots of hugs!

"What are you going to buy, Hannah?" Nancy asked from the back seat, where she sat between Bess and George.

"When at a goat farm . . . buy goat cheese!" Hannah declared, turning off the engine. "I heard the flavor of the day is blueberry pecan."

"Blueberry pecan?" Bess said with surprise. "Is that cheese or a yummy cookie?"

Hannah and the girls climbed out of the car. Nancy always liked taking the receipt card from the farm's parking meter and sticking it behind the windshield wipers. It had the date and time on it.

"Do you have your yoga mats?" Hannah asked.

"Check," Nancy said, lifting her rolled-up mat.

"My hot pink mat matches my leggings," Bess said with a smile. "In case you haven't noticed."

"How can we not, Bess?" George groaned. "They're so bright, even the goats will need sunglasses!"

Nancy giggled. Bess and George were cousins, but as different as different could be. Bess had blond hair, blue eyes, and wore the trendiest clothes. Dark-haired George only wore her comfiest jeans—and had the holey knees to prove it!

After waving goodbye to Hannah, the girls headed to the goat pen. On the way, they saw production trucks, television equipment, and a long table filled with snack foods for the crew of *Wake Up, River Heights*.

"Omigosh!" Bess gasped. "Do you see what I see?"

"Chocolate donuts with rainbow sprinkles!" George said, smiling at the table. "Maybe they'll let us have some."

"Not the donuts, George," Bess said. "The kids! *Human* kids!"

Nancy looked where Bess was pointing. Laying down yoga mats inside the goat pen were several of their friends and classmates!

"They showed up after all!" Nancy said happily.

The girls high-fived before joining the others in the pen. The goats were there too, busy grazing in their open goat shed.

Sophie greeted the kids, then introduced them to the yoga instructor, Eddie Finch. Eddie wore zebra-striped yoga wear as he waved to the class.

Next, Sophie introduced Bev, the director, and one of the show's hosts, Stephanie Burns. Stephanie was too busy putting on lip gloss to say hi or wave. Suddenly—

"Okay, quiet, everyone," Bev called out as she listened closely through her headset. "Ready in five . . . counting down."

Nancy reached out to squeeze Bess's hand. *This is it!*

"Five . . . four . . . three," Bev counted back, "two—"

She pointed to Stephanie, who flashed a glossy bright smile at the camera before beginning to speak.

"Most kids spend spring break on playdates or seeing the latest blockbuster movie. But these kids spend them with other kids. Goats!"

The goats bleated softly as they meandered out of the shed toward the giggling kids.

"Don't tell the goats, but our first pose is the lion!" Eddie joked. "Everyone, kneel on your mats and sit way back on your heels."

Like the others, Nancy kneeled on her mat. By now most of the goats were playfully scampering around the posing kids. Some were jumping onto their backs, but all of the goats were very gentle. All except one . . .

"*Baaaaa!*" one goat screamed as he raced around the pen, bouncing up and down on kids and chewing everything in sight!

"He chewed on my sneaker!" one girl complained.

"He's pulling my yoga mat out from under me!" a boy shouted as the goat tugged the mat between his teeth. "Get him to stop!"

"*Baaaaa!*"

The gentle goats backed away as the out-of-control goat charged toward Kendra's water bottle. He grabbed it between his teeth and swung it through the air. Kids shrieked as water splashed everywhere!

"What's up with this goat?" George shouted.

Nancy had no idea—until she spotted something on the goat's side. Something she knew she had seen before!

Chapter

SILLY BILLY

"Bess, George!" Nancy called. "Check out the brown star-shaped mark on the goat's side."

"Holy guacamole!" George said, staring at the spot. "That goat's Pogo!"

Shrieks and bleats filled the air as Pogo continued to charge through the pen. Eddie grumbled as he rolled up his yoga mat. "I may be wearing zebra stripes, but I'm no zookeeper!"

Bev was pointing frantically to the camera. Stephanie jumped in front of it, forcing a smile.

"I guess this is what happens when good goats go baaaaaaad. Heh-heh. Back to you in the studio!"

George shook her head as Pogo continued to run amok. "I knew I should have played soccer instead," she groaned.

Sophie led a team of farm workers into the pen. After chasing Pogo for a few minutes, one was able to catch him and hold him gently.

"That is not a Sweet Creams Farm goat," Sophie said, pointing to Pogo. "I didn't see him when I came into the pen at six thirty this morning."

Nancy, Bess, and George exchanged a look before hurrying over to Sophie.

"He's not one of your goats, Sophie," Nancy explained. "He's Pogo the Trampoline Goat."

"He belongs to the Disher family on Magnolia Street," George added.

"Magnolia Street is just up the hill," Sophie told the farm worker holding Pogo. "Could you please look up the Dishers' house number and return their goat?"

"Baaaa!" Pogo bleated as he was carried out of the pen.

The other kids grumbled as they rolled up their yoga mats.

"My mat is covered with goat spit," Marcy Ruben complained. "Gross."

"That nutty goat pulled out my sneaker lace." Peter Patino groaned. "And I'm wearing high-tops!"

"So . . . you didn't like the class?" George asked.

"Here's what I thought of the class, Georgia Fayne!" Madison Foley said, holding her thumb down.

Nancy could see George frown—she hated her real name. But Madison wasn't the only one who was disappointed.

"You promised us gentle goats, Nancy," Kendra said. "Not crazy trampoline goats."

Nancy felt awful, but she knew it wasn't her fault. She also knew what had to be done. . . .

"I have no idea how Pogo got here," Nancy

admitted, "but I promise that the Clue Crew will find out!"

After the kids quietly left the pen, Bess and George turned to Nancy.

"A promise is serious stuff, Nancy," George said.

"How are we going to find out how Pogo got into the yoga class?" Bess asked.

Nancy smiled as she reached into the pocket of her hoodie. "Luckily, Pogo didn't chew up my clue book!"

She carried her clue book everywhere—even to goat yoga. It's where the Clue Crew wrote all of their suspects and clues for each new case. Tucked between the pages was Nancy's favorite purple-ink pen.

The Clue Crew got to work. Nancy turned to a clean page in her clue book, where she wrote *Case: Pogo Puzzler.*

"How did Pogo get inside the pen in the first place?" Nancy asked.

"Somebody must have brought him," Bess said.

"He couldn't have walked here all by himself."

"Sophie didn't notice Pogo at six thirty this morning, when the farm opened," George pointed out. "He was probably snuck into the pen between then and our yoga class at seven thirty."

"The TV crew was here early," Nancy said. "Wouldn't they have seen someone sneak Pogo in?"

"Not if they were busy," George said.

"Plus, there's only one gate that opens into the pen," Bess pointed out, "and it's right in the front."

"Unless there's another gate somewhere," Nancy said, shutting her clue book. "Come on. Let's investi-*gate*!"

Starting at the gate, the girls walked around the pen. The front was always grassy, but the back was muddy.

"Great," Bess complained. "How am I going to keep my new sneakers clean with all this mud?"

"Walk on your hands," George teased.

Bess glared at her cousin. "Very funny."

Nancy, Bess, and George walked alongside

the fence until they found another gate. It was smaller than the one at the front of the pen, but still a gate!

"Look what I found," George said, pointing to the muddy ground. "Animal tracks leading through the gate inside."

"They look like tiny goat hooves," Nancy said. "But how do we know they're Pogo's?"

Bess touched a strip of purple paper stuck to the gate. "Whoever opened the gate lost this," she said. "It's a purple Pogo bracelet!"

Nancy removed the paper bracelet from the door. To keep it safe, she placed it between the pages of her clue book like a bookmark. "Good

clue, Bess," she said. "Next, let's figure out who brought Pogo to goat yoga and why!"

"To ruin the class?" Bess guessed.

"Or to get rid of Pogo," George suggested with a frown, "like Leslie Disher wanted to do."

"Leslie was mad at Pogo for chewing up her Brad Sylvester poster," Nancy agreed. "She wished Pogo would get lost."

Georgia scratched her head. "Maybe Leslie made her own wish come true by walking Pogo here and leaving him?"

"Leslie had a purple Pogo bracelet too," Bess added. "Just like the one we found on the fence."

"But Quincy must have handed out a lot of those," George said.

Quincy! The name made Nancy look up from her clue book.

"Quincy said he wanted Pogo to be on TV," Nancy said. "Maybe Quincy snuck Pogo into the goat pen this morning!"

"Why wouldn't Quincy stick around to watch?" Bess asked. "Or brag that he was Pogo's manager?"

"Quincy could have seen Pogo go bonkers," George suggested, "and took off so he wouldn't be blamed."

Nancy added Quincy's name to their suspect list.

"We should look for Hannah in case she wants to leave," Nancy said as she closed her clue book. "At least we'll be leaving with two good clues and two suspects."

"And two muddy sneakers." Bess sighed, frowning down at her feet. "Great."

On the way to the market, the girls walked by the parking lot. Nancy could see a woman climbing into a bright blue car—a woman she had seen just yesterday.

"You guys," Nancy said in almost a whisper, "do you see what I see?"

"See what?" George asked.

"Our third suspect," Nancy said with a smile.

Chapter

SOUR PICKLES

The woman in the blue car reached out to shut the door. Nancy, Bess, and George stood still as they watched her pull out of the parking lot.

"That was Nina Pickles, wasn't it?" George asked as the car drove off.

"Why would Nina come back to the farm?" Bess asked. "Especially after Sophie said she couldn't show off her new kids' clothes for the TV filming?"

"Maybe to ruin the goat yoga class this morning!" Nancy replied.

George shook her head. "I don't know, Nancy. How would Nina even know about Pogo or where to get him?"

"And that bracelet we found on the fence is so not her style," Bess added.

Nancy agreed with them both. She wrote Nina's name in her clue book along with a question mark.

"We still have two suspects," Nancy said. "Two and a half!"

The girls found Hannah drinking a cup of coffee by the farm's snack truck. When she heard what had happened during the yoga class, her eyes popped wide open.

"I had no idea!" she said, glancing down at two shopping bags at her side. "I was too busy buying goat yogurt and cheese."

"Blueberry pecan goat cheese?" Nancy asked hopefully.

"No," Hannah said. "The man selling the cheeses told me someone bought all of the blueberry pecan logs. I bought cranberry walnut instead."

Nancy, Bess, and George walked with Hannah to the car. After helping to load the bags into the trunk, Nancy removed the parking card and handed it to Hannah.

When everyone was buckled in, Hannah asked, "Are we all going home now?"

"Actually, could you please drive us to Magnolia Street?" Nancy asked.

"What's on Magnolia Street?"

"That's where the Dishers live," Nancy explained. "We want to talk to Leslie Disher about Pogo."

"And read her journal," George added quickly.

Nancy turned to stare at George. "Her journal? Why do you want to read her journal?"

"If Leslie writes everything in her journal," George explained, "she might have written her plans for Pogo."

"No way, George. We can't do that!" Bess said. "Reading journals is snooping!"

"We're detectives, Bess," George insisted. "Snooping is our business!"

The Disher house was up the road, and only four blocks from the Drews'. Hannah dropped the girls off, and they promised that they'd walk home together.

In front of the house, Nancy said, "I heard a *baaaa*. Sounds like Pogo's back home."

Nancy, Bess, and George followed the bleats to the backyard, where they saw Pogo. This time he was not on the trampoline. Instead, he stood by Wesley, drinking from a bottle.

"Hi, Wesley," Nancy said. "You heard what happened with Pogo, right?"

"Sure did. But I have no idea how Pogo got into that goat yoga class."

"Then I guess somebody got your goat," George joked before earning an elbow nudge from Bess.

"Is your sister here?" Nancy asked Wesley. "We'd like to say hi."

"Leslie just got home. You can go upstairs to her room. The side door is unlocked."

Nancy, Bess, and George filed through the side door into the house. They gave a little wave to Mrs. Disher, who was sitting in her office, before climbing the stairs.

"Keep your eyes out for clues that Leslie was at Sweet Creams this morning," Nancy whispered.

"What kind of clues?" George asked.

Bess groaned. "Muddy sneakers."

When the girls reached the second floor, they spotted a door plastered with Brad Sylvester pictures.

"I'll take a wild guess that this is Leslie's room," George said, heading to the door. She knocked twice, then called, "Leslie? It's George."

"Nancy and Bess too!" Nancy called through the door.

They waited about ten seconds. No answer.

"Maybe Leslie didn't hear us," Bess said. "She's probably listening to Brad Sylvester tunes through her earbuds."

"Then I'm going in," George said, turning the doorknob.

"Don't, George," Nancy whispered. "Wait—"

Too late. The Brad Sylvester pictures fluttered in the breeze as George swung the door open. Nancy and Bess followed her inside. They didn't see Leslie—but they recognized someone else!

"OMG!" Nancy gasped, not believing her eyes.

"It's him! It's him!" Bess cried. "It's Brad Sylvester!"

Chapter

5

PRIVATE EYES

Nancy, Bess, and George stared ahead, open-mouthed. Brad stood with his pearly toothed smile in the middle of Leslie's room. Until he fell forward with a *PLUNK!*

"Brad?" Bess asked quietly.

The girls stared down at a pancake-flat Brad Sylvester, facedown on the floor.

"It's one of those life-size cardboard cutouts." Nancy sighed with disappointment. "The breeze from the closing door must have knocked it down."

George looked around the room. "This place is on Brad overdrive," she said. "Brad Sylvester bedspread, Brad curtains, bobblehead Brad on the windowsill—"

"We already found tons of Brad," Nancy cut in. "Let's find clues that Leslie was at Sweet Creams Farm this morning."

"If Leslie brought Pogo to the farm," Bess said, "how did she get him there?"

"In that!" George said, pointing.

On top of Leslie's desk was a big duffel bag. "Leslie carried Pogo to the farm in a bag?" Nancy asked.

"Why not?" George asked, reaching for the bag. "Let's see if it smells like goat inside."

"Let's not!" Bess wrinkled her nose. "That's gross, George!"

George was already grabbing the open bag by its handle.

It slipped out of her hand, dropped to the floor, and landed on its side.

"Oops," George said as the bag's contents spilled out. A toothbrush, hairbrush, scrunchie, slippers, and a nightshirt scattered across the floor.

Nancy took a moment to study the stuff, then said, "Leslie could not have been at the farm early this morning."

"Why not?" Bess asked.

"This is all sleepover stuff," Nancy explained.

"Leslie was probably at an all-night sleepover."

"How do we know it was last night?" Bess asked. "She could have gone two nights ago and not have unpacked."

"We can check if her toothbrush is still wet," George suggested.

"Eww, George," Bess exclaimed. "That's even grosser than sniffing for goat."

But George was already on to something else. She pulled a notebook from the bag. On the cover was a heart-shaped Brad Sylvester sticker. "Look what I found!" she said. "This has got to be Leslie's journal!"

"Step away from my journal!" a voice commanded. "I repeat—step away from my journal!"

The girls spun around. Standing in the doorway was Leslie, and she looked mad!

"What are you doing in my room?" Leslie demanded. "Were you going to snoop through my journal?"

"No," George said. "I was just going to read it."

With a shriek, Leslie snatched the notebook

away. "Nobody reads my journal except me. Or Brad Sylvester, because half of it is about him anyway."

Nancy gave her friends a sideways glance. The only defense they had left now was the truth. . . .

"Someone snuck Pogo in our goat yoga class this morning," Nancy explained. "We were just trying to find out who did it."

"You thought it was me?" Leslie cried. "Why?"

"You wanted Pogo gone, Leslie," Bess said. "We heard you with our own ears."

Leslie sighed as she placed her journal on her

desk. "I know what Pogo did at the yoga class, but I didn't put him there."

"But you were mad at Pogo for chewing up your things," Nancy said, "like your Brad Sylvester poster."

"Sure, but I would never get rid of Wesley's pet. Anyway," she said, pointing at her spilled duffel bag, "I was at Nikki Pelligrino's sleepover last night."

"Or," George said slowly, "maybe you just put that sleepover bag there so we would think you were at a sleepover!"

"Huh?" Leslie asked.

"You guys," Bess whispered, "Leslie *was* at a sleepover last night."

"How do you know?" Nancy whispered.

"Look at her red eyes from no sleep," Bess pointed out. "I know sleepover eyes when I see them."

"And," Nancy said, glancing down at Leslie's feet, "her sneakers are clean as a whistle. No mud."

"She's also wearing her purple Pogo bracelet,"

George said, "so she couldn't have lost it at the farm."

"Hello? I'm standing right here. And it's not a Pogo bracelet," Leslie said, raising her wrist. "It's a Brad Sylvester bracelet with a bunch of tiny hearts next to his name. See?"

Nancy moved closer for a better look. The bracelet did have Brad's name, not Pogo's. It had tiny hearts, too. "Oh," she said.

Leslie smiled. "While you're here, let me show you my wickedly awesome Brad Sylvester things."

Leslie lifted a jar from her desk and held it up.

"Eww!" Bess said, eyeing the bluish clumpy wad inside. "Is that chewed-up gum in there?"

"Not just anyone's gum," Leslie said. "Brad chewed it up and spit it out on the sidewalk after a concert. I was lucky to see it and scrape it off—"

"We get it, Leslie. Thanks!" George cut in.

"That's even grosser than the wet toothbrush," Bess whispered to Nancy and George. "Can we leave now?"

Nancy, Bess, and George helped Leslie pick

up her spilled things—except for the toothbrush. They thanked her for being honest, then said goodbye and left.

"At least Pogo is back home," Nancy said as they walked away from the Disher house. She slowed down to cross Leslie's name off their suspect list.

"We have one suspect left," Bess said. "Quincy Taylor."

"One and a half," Nancy pointed out. "We saw Nina Pickles at the farm today, remember?"

"Speaking of pickles," George said with a grin, "my mom catered a sweet sixteen last night and has a ton of leftovers. Let's go to my house for some lunch."

"Thanks, George!" Nancy said.

"I'm so glad my aunt is a caterer!" Bess said with a smile.

Nancy, Bess, and George walked straight to the Fayne house. Mrs. Fayne was glad to feed them chicken wings, pigs in a blanket, and green salad.

But as Nancy ate, the case was still on her

mind. "Mrs. Fayne?" she asked. "Have you ever shopped at Nina Pickles's store?"

"No," Mrs. Fayne said, "but I catered Nina's birthday party a few months ago."

"At her store, Aunt Louise?" Bess asked.

"At her home," Mrs. Fayne replied. "It's the cutest little house on Magnolia Street!"

Magnolia Street?

All three girls stared at Mrs. Fayne.

"We were just on Magnolia Street, Mom," George said. "Wesley and Leslie Disher live there."

"Someone else lives on Magnolia Street," Nancy said as a new thought clicked into place. "Pogo the Trampoline Goat!"

Chapter

SAY CHEESE!

"Nancy, are you thinking what I'm thinking?" Bess asked excitedly.

Nancy nodded. "If Nina lives nears the Dishers, she probably knows about Pogo!"

"She's close enough to have taken Pogo too!" George said. "I think Nina Pickles went from being half a suspect to a whole suspect."

Mrs. Fayne smiled as she poured the girls more juice. "Sounds like the Clue Crew is working on another case."

"And we're about to crack it wide open." George looked up at her mom. "Is it okay if we use your computer? I want to look up some stuff about Nina Pickles."

"Sure," Mrs. Fayne said with a grin. "After you wash all that sticky barbecue sauce off your hands."

After lunch, and with clean hands, the Clue Crew huddled around Mrs. Fayne's computer. A computer geek and proud of it, George tapped the keys. A few seconds later, Nina's website filled the screen.

Nancy leaned over for a better look. "It says Nina is having a special event today."

"It's a fashion show two hours from now for Nina's new line of kids' clothes," Bess said excitedly. "Cool!"

The girls read all about the fashion show. It would be held at Gym Dandy, a gym just for kids. Admission was free.

"We should go there and question Nina," Nancy said.

"How can we do that in the middle of a fashion show?" George asked. "Once she finds out we're detectives, her lips will be zipped!"

"Ooh, I know!" Bess exclaimed.

"What?" Nancy and George asked at the same time.

"We'll go there as *reporters*," Bess said. "Fashion reporters. We'll wear dark sunglasses and hats so Nina won't recognize us from the farm."

"I don't know," George said. "What do I know about fashion?"

"Nothing," Bess admitted, "so you stay quiet while Nancy and I do the talking."

"We should start by asking her fashion questions," Nancy said, "and little by little . . . Pogo questions!"

"Let's go to my house," Bess said. "We can go through my clothes and accessories for disguises."

"*All* your clothes and accessories?" George cried. "We only have two hours, Bess!"

"Ha-ha," Bess said, not laughing.

The Clue Crew rushed to the Marvins' house,

where they picked out outfits. Nancy and Bess paired jackets with dressy pants, topping them off with hats and sunglasses. George stuck to jeans and a black faux-leather jacket.

"No accessories, George?" Bess asked.

"*Boom!*" George said, picking up her phone. "To record Nina's answers. We're reporters now, remember?"

Nancy, Bess, and George hurried to Gym Dandy. They had no trouble getting into the kids' gym, where the fashion show was already going strong.

"Omigosh!" Bess whispered. "There's a real-life runway!"

Nancy watched as kids their age strutted up and down the long, narrow runway in Nina Pickles's designs. On both sides of the runway, guests sat enjoying the show.

"Remember, we're not here to watch the fashion show," Nancy reminded her friends. "We're here to ask Nina about Pogo."

"What are we waiting for?" George said. "There she is!"

Nancy turned to see Nina just a few feet away.

"Ms. Pickles, Ms. Pickles!" Nancy called as she, Bess, and George ran toward her. "May we ask you a few questions, please?"

Nina raised an eyebrow at the girls. "Questions?" she asked. "What kind of questions?"

"Fashion questions," Nancy said. "We're reporters from . . . from—"

"From *Trendy Tween* magazine!" Bess blurted. "We'd like to know about your new line of active-wear just for kids like us."

"A magazine?" Nina asked excitedly. "I only have a few minutes, but go ahead. What would you like to know?"

George held up her phone to record while Nancy asked the first question: "Ms. Pickles, why do you think kids will like your new line of activewear?"

"What's not to like?" Nina chuckled. "My kids' activewear is colorful, fun, and most important—comfy!"

"Comfy?" Bess repeated. "Are you saying your yoga pants—"

"Next question!" George cut in. "Nina, were you disappointed when Sophie Sweet wouldn't show your clothes on *Wake Up, River Heights* this morning?"

"George!" Nancy groaned under her breath. They were supposed to get to the goat topic slowly!

Nina blinked, surprised at the sudden question. Then she said, "Sure, I was disappointed. But not anymore."

"Why not?" all three girls asked in unison.

"Because I got something to make up for it," Nina said with a grin. "And it was totally worth it!"

Nina glanced over at the busy runway. "I'd better get back to my fashion show. Thanks for the questions, girls!"

When Nina walked out of earshot, Nancy, Bess, and George huddled to discuss what they'd found out.

"What do you think Nina got?" Nancy asked.

"Revenge?" Bess suggested, her eyes wide.

"Oh, girls," a singsong voice called.

Nancy, Bess, and George looked up to see a woman wearing a headset and walking in their direction. "Hi. I'm Poppy, the director of the fashion show," she said like she was in a rush. "You're the three girls who came together to model, right?"

Nancy was about to say no when Bess blurted out, "Right!"

"What?" George whispered angrily, but Poppy was already yanking clothing off a rack.

"Here are the outfits you'll be modeling,"

Poppy said. "Put them on behind the screen, then hurry out to the runway." She dropped an outfit into each girl's arms.

As she walked away, George shook her head. "No way. The only modeling I do is with clay!"

"Please, George," Bess said. "It'll be fun."

Nancy thought so too, even though she wanted to keep working on their case. She looked down at the outfit in her arms. "This hoodie is nice, but I can't wear yoga pants," she said. "There're no pocket for my clue book!"

Nancy, Bess, and George filed behind the screen. The first thing they saw back there was another rack filled with clothes. The next thing was a long table filled with food. Each platter was covered with cellophane.

"It's probably for the after-party," Bess said. "I hope we can have some."

Nancy peered through the clear cellophane at the food. There were crackers, dip, raw veggies, and a platter of log-shaped white things. Propped up near the platter was a small chalkboard sign that read: GOAT CHEESE: BLUEBERRY PECAN!

"Blueberry pecan!" Nancy exclaimed.

"What about it?" Bess asked.

"That was the flavor of the day at Sweet Creams Farm today," Nancy explained. "Hannah said someone bought all of the logs!"

"So?" George asked.

"So maybe Nina didn't come to the farm with Pogo," Nancy said. "Maybe she came . . . with a *shopping list*!"

Chapter

7

WHEELS AND SQUEALS

"A shopping list?" George asked.

"What do you mean, Nancy?" Bess asked.

"Nina could have been at Sweet Creams Farm this morning to buy cheese!" Nancy said, nodding at the table. "This goat cheese."

"Nina still could have snuck Pogo into the goat pen before she went shopping," George pointed out.

"She seems like a multitasker," Bess added.

"You've got five minutes, girls!" Poppy called

from the other side of the screen. "And don't forget the sneakers!"

The girls looked down to see three pairs of brand-new sneakers lined up beneath the rack.

"We only have enough time to put on the hoodies and the sneakers," Nancy said. "Let's get dressed."

"And get this over with," George muttered.

When they were ready, Nancy, Bess, and George lined up behind the screen.

"Hurry, girls. Hurry!" Poppy called, pointing to the runway. "You're on!"

"Just do what I do," Bess shouted over the loud, pulsating music. "And don't forget to pivot."

A colorful balloon arch led to the runway. Nancy, Bess, and George stood under it, striking glam poses. They were about to step forward when Poppy ran over, calling, "Wait! The sneakers aren't switched on yet."

"What's not switched on?" Nancy asked.

"The wheels!" Poppy replied. "Off you go!"

Poppy gave each girl a gentle push.

"Ahhhhhhhhh!" Nancy cried out as she began sliding down the runway. "These are *roller sneakers*!"

"I can't stop!" Bess cried as she slip-slided too. "George, what do we do?"

"I don't know!" George shouted as her feet moved in opposite directions. "I've never worn sneakers with wheels before!"

All three friends zigzagged up and down the runway. To keep from falling, Nancy and Bess grabbed the arch. Balloons popped loudly as they burst. Guests shrieked and jumped up as George swerved toward their chairs. She spun around and landed on an empty chair, her feet kicking up in the air.

"Whoa." She groaned under her breath.

"Thank you, girls. Thank yooooooou!" Nina shouted, rushing down the runway. She smiled nervously at the guests. "I guess that brings new meaning to the words 'fashion forward'!"

When no one laughed, Nina blurted, "That concludes our show. All outfits are available at my store starting today. Buh-bye!"

Guests filed out of Gym Dandy, some shaking their heads in disbelief. Nancy, Bess, and George sat on the runway, pulling off their sneakers while Nina argued with Poppy.

"Why were those girls on the runway?" Nina demanded. "They're reporters, not models."

Poppy apologized, then raced to stop the popped balloon arch from toppling over. Happy to be out of the rollaway sneakers, the girls stepped into their own shoes. They then walked over to Nina.

"Actually, Ms. Pickles, we're detectives," Nancy explained.

"The Clue Crew," Bess added. "We were trying to find out who put Pogo in the yoga class this morning."

George folded her arms across her chest. "You do know Pogo, don't you, Ms. Pickles?" she asked. "Pogo the Trampoline Goat, who lives on your block?"

"Of course, I know the Dishers' pet goat," Nina said, "but I would do nothing of the kind."

"You were mad at Sophie Sweet because your new line of children's clothes wouldn't be shown on TV," Nancy said.

"I told you before," Nina said, "Sophie offered me something to make up for it—lots of goat cheese free of charge for my after-show party."

"Oh," Nancy said.

"You see," Nina went on, "I needed snacks to serve all the guests."

"But you just sent everybody home," Bess said.

Nina's eyes widened. "I did, didn't I?" she said. Then she shouted, "Poppy! What are we going to do with all that cheese?"

While Nina darted over to Poppy, the girls pulled off their hoodies and hung them on a nearby rack.

"Modeling is harder than I thought." Bess sighed. "But at least we got to question Nina."

"We still don't know if Nina told us the truth, though," George said. "So what if she got free cheese at the farm? She still could have done something cheesy!"

Nancy wasn't ready to cross Nina off her suspect list either. That was until they went outside and saw Nina's car. . . .

"Look!" Nancy said, pointing to a card stuck behind the windshield wipers. "It's a parking receipt from Sweet Creams Farm. Nina forgot to take it off."

"What about it?" Bess asked.

"It shows the time Nina got to Sweet Creams Farm," Nancy explained. She stood on her tiptoes to read the receipt. "She got to the farm at seven forty-five."

"Pogo was already in our yoga class by then," Bess said.

"Nina couldn't have brought Pogo to the farm in the morning," George added. "She really did just come to pick up all that cheese."

"Which means she's no longer a suspect," Nancy said as she crossed Nina's name off the list.

"Quincy is our last suspect," George said. "Should we question him next?"

Nancy shook her head as she shut her clue book.

"I have to go home now," she said. "My dad and I are going for a special spring break night out."

"What are you going to do?" George asked.

Nancy giggled as she remembered the roll-away sneakers. "Anything but roller skate!"

"They serve pizza with spinach and kale here, Daddy," Nancy said, pointing to the chalkboard menu above their booth. "That's one way to eat your veggies!"

Nancy and her dad were having dinner at a new pizza place called Sugar and Slice. Each pie came with a yummy ice-cream sundae for dessert.

Mr. Drew put down his slice to pull out his phone. "Before I forget," he said, "I thought you might want to see this."

Nancy swallowed her last piece of pizza crust. "See what?" she asked.

"This video." Mr. Drew held up his phone. "It seems to be going viral."

Nancy leaned over the table for a closer look. What she saw made her jaw drop. It was a video

of Pogo in their yoga class from that morning!

"That's me!" Nancy gasped when she saw herself on the screen. Shrieks and bleats accompanied the frenzied yoga class as she and her friends tried to dodge the upset kids. "Daddy, this is so embarrassing."

A close shot of Pogo suddenly filled the screen. For the first time, Nancy noticed something around his neck.

"Pause the video, please!" Nancy said. "I think I see something."

"What?" Mr. Drew asked.

"A clue!"

Chapter

PET FRET

After Mr. Drew paused the video, Nancy pointed to a collar around Pogo's neck. It was green with white polka dots.

"Pogo wasn't wearing a collar when we first met him," Nancy said. "I'll bet that collar has a matching leash that snaps on to it."

"I'm not sure where you're going with this," Mr. Drew admitted. "What does Pogo's collar have to do with your case?"

Nancy loved sharing the Clue Crew's latest

mysteries with her father. Mr. Drew was a lawyer, and he knew a thing or two about cases.

"Someone must have walked Pogo to the farm," Nancy explained, "just like someone would walk a dog." She pointed to the collar. "So that's what we have to look for when we visit Quincy tomorrow—a matching green leash with white polka dots!"

"Remember to ask Quincy lots of questions before you accuse him of anything," Mr. Drew said, placing his phone back in his pocket. "Sometimes your last suspect is not really your last one."

Nancy reached for another slice of pizza. "Just like my last slice wasn't my last either!" she said with a grin.

"I can't believe someone had a camera yesterday!" Bess groaned the next morning after watching the Pogo video. "My hair was such a mess!"

George rolled her eyes as she pocketed her phone. "Bess, the whole place was a mess after Pogo got finished with it."

"Now that you know what Pogo's collar looks like," Nancy said, "let's go to Quincy's house to see if he has the matching leash."

The Clue Crew had met in front of the Drews' house before heading to Quincy's. They were about to start walking when—

"Spring has sprung. Spring has sprung! *Raaaaak!*"

Nancy would know that squawky voice anywhere. It was their friend Shelby Metcalf's pet parrot, Ernie!

Shelby walked over with Ernie perched on her arm. "Hey, Clue Crew," she said. "Where are you guys going?"

"To Quincy's house," Bess answered.

"What a coinky-dink!" Shelby exclaimed. "Ernie and I are going there too."

"You are?" Nancy asked. "Why?"

"Because Quincy is having auditions," Shelby explained. "He's looking for new animal acts to manage."

"It's . . . showtiiiiiime!" Ernie screeched. *"Arrrk!"*

"New animal acts?" George asked. "Isn't managing a trampoline goat enough?"

"Raaak!" Ernie squawked. "Bad vibes!"

"I know," Nancy said with a smile. "Why don't we all walk to Quincy's house together?"

"Um . . . I don't think you guys can go to Quincy's house today," Shelby said.

"Why not?" Nancy asked.

"Quincy told me that only kids with talented pets are invited to the audition. As you know, Ernie sings."

"Raaaaaaaaaak!" Ernie screeched loudly.

"You call *that* singing?" George asked.

"Sure," Shelby said with a shrug. "Even Brad Sylvester has to clear his throat."

The girls watched Shelby quietly as she walked down the block with Ernie.

"We'll never get to question Quincy today," Bess grumbled. "Or look for the green leash with white polka dots."

"All because of those singing, dancing pets." George frowned.

"Pets!" Nancy gasped as a new idea popped into her head. "I have a talented pet too. My puppy Chocolate Chip can roll a ball with her nose!"

"Which means Chip can audition!" Bess said excitedly.

"And while Chip is wowing Quincy," George said, "I'll search for that green leash with white polka dots!"

"Will Chip be okay around all those other pets, Nancy?" Bess asked.

"Yes," Nancy said with confidence. "The only animals that make Chip go wild are squirrels, and who has a squirrel for a pet?"

George hurried home to get her lucky soccer ball for Chip to roll. Nancy and Bess went inside the Drew house to get Chip ready for her audition.

Less than an hour later, the girls and Chip were heading to Quincy's house. The frisky chocolate Lab was already rolling George's ball down the block.

When they reached Quincy's, George whistled through her teeth. "Wow!" she exclaimed. "Who knew so many kids in River Heights had pets?"

The Taylors' front yard was crowded with cats, more dogs, a hamster in a cage, a rabbit, and of course, Ernie!

Kevin Garcia from school was there. He held a cage covered with a thick cloth. The girls were curious what was underneath.

"Who's your secret pet, Kevin?" Nancy asked.

"His name is Toffee," Kevin said, "but no peeking until he performs."

All eyes turned to Quincy as he hopped up on a plastic milk crate. "Welcome to the auditions, everyone," he announced. "As you all know by now, I was Pogo the Trampoline Goat's manager."

"*Was* his manager?" Nancy whispered to Bess and George. "Isn't he *still* Pogo's manager?"

"Whoever wins this audition," Quincy went on, "gets to be represented by me."

"Oh, blah, blah, blah," George whispered. "While the other pets audition, let's look for that leash."

"Good idea," Nancy whispered.

"Wait!" Bess said. "Quincy just called Kevin up first. I want to see what kind of a pet he has!"

"Introducing," Kevin shouted as he whipped the cloth off the cage, "Toffee!"

Kevin opened the cage door. Gasps filled the yard when a tiny gray creature with a long tail peeked out. The creature gazed at the crowd with big round eyes—then jumped out of his cage!

"*Woof, woof, woof!*" Chip barked loudly.

Using both hands, Nancy clutched Chip's leash to hold her back. But it was no use. Chip shot straight at Toffee, who was gliding through the air!

"Oh noooo!" Nancy cried. "Kevin's secret pet is a *flying squirrel*!"

Chapter

9

CHEW CLUE

Pet cats hissed and raised their hackles while Chip kept barking, and the other dogs joined her. The hamster jumped frantically in her cage, and Ernie, still on Shelby's shoulder, flapped his wings, squawking, "Naughty dog, naughty dog! Oooh boy!"

Chip pulled Nancy all the way to where Kevin was standing. Toffee had climbed up onto his shoulder, his eyes wide and his fur ruffled.

"See what your dog did, Nancy?" Kevin said. "She scared Toffee!"

"Sorry," Nancy said, holding Chip firmly by her collar, "but no one expected to see a pet squirrel!"

"Toffee is *not* a squirrel!" Kevin insisted. "He's a sugar glider."

"A sugar glider?" Bess repeated.

"Is that a pet—or a candy bar?" George said.

"A sugar glider is a marsupial," Kevin explained as he gently petted Toffee. "Sort of like a teeny-tiny kangaroo."

Quincy stepped up to Kevin. "What does your sugar glider do?" he asked. "Any tricks? Can he fly through hoops or hop like a kangaroo?"

"No," Kevin said. "He's just a neat pocket pet."

"Then put him in your pocket," Quincy snapped. He turned to Nancy. "Take your dog home, please. She'll never make it in Hollywood!"

Nancy didn't want to leave without asking Quincy about Pogo's leash. By then Chip had calmed down, but the other pets were still jumpy.

Quincy had no choice but to call off the pet auditions.

Nancy, Bess, and George watched the other kids carry and walk their pets away from the Taylor house. The owners were disappointed, but not as disappointed as Quincy.

"Phooey ka-blooey," he said. "Now I'll never get to see Harriet the Hula-Hoop Hamster."

"Sorry again, Quincy," Nancy said. "But we didn't come for the auditions. We're trying to get answers on our latest case."

"What case?" Quincy asked.

"Someone put Pogo in our goat yoga class yesterday," George explained. "Was it you?"

Quincy shook his head. "No way. Why would I put a trampoline goat in a yoga class?"

"You told us you wanted Pogo to be on television," Bess said, "and you're his manager."

"*Was* his manager!" Quincy sighed. "Two days ago, Wesley fired me. He said he didn't want Pogo to be a famous trampoline goat anymore."

"Fired?" Nancy said, puzzled. "Then you didn't

take Pogo to Sweet Creams Farm yesterday so he could be on *Wake Up, River Heights*?"

"Why bother if I'm not Pogo's manager anymore?" Quincy asked glumly. "Besides, I was watching *Danger Dog* then. I watch it at that time every morning."

"*Danger Dog*!" Bess said, her eyes lighting up. "We heard that yesterday's episode was awesome. Do you remember what it was?"

"How could I forget?" Quincy said with a smile. "It was the flea circus episode. It's the best!"

He picked up a stick and tossed it for Chip to fetch. While they played, Bess whispered excitedly to Nancy and George, "You guys, Quincy is right. Henderson told us the flea circus episode would be on!"

She shook her head, adding, "Quincy couldn't have been at the farm yesterday morning, because he was home watching *Danger Dog*."

"Danger Dog saves the day!" George declared.

"At least for Quincy," Nancy said with a smile.

The Clue Crew thanked Quincy for his help;

then Nancy walked Chip out of the yard along with Bess and George.

"I'm glad Quincy's not a suspect anymore," Nancy said. "But I'm not glad that he was our *last* suspect."

George held on to Chip's leash while Nancy crossed Quincy's name off the suspect list. She was about to close the book when the purple Pogo bracelet tucked inside fell out.

"I'll get it," Bess said, picking up the bracelet and handing it back to Nancy. Before Nancy could slip it back into her clue book, she saw something that she hadn't noticed before. . . .

Nancy gasped "Bess, George, I just found a clue on our clue!"

She pointed to two little ragged marks on the bracelet. "My hand must have covered them when I pulled this bracelet off the fence."

"Maybe they're rips from the fence," George said.

"Rips would be longish," Nancy said. "These look like teeth marks."

"Teeth marks?" Bess exclaimed.

"Whose teeth?" George asked.

"Pogo's!" Nancy said. "He was chewing on Wesley's purple bracelet the day before the yoga class, remember?"

"I remember," Bess said. "But if the bracelet was Wesley's, and we found it on the fence—"

"Why would Wesley sneak his own goat into the yoga class?" George cut in.

"There's only one way to find out," Nancy said as she closed her clue book. "Next stop, the Disher house!"

Clue Crew—and
YOU!

Can you solve the Pogo puzzler? Try thinking like the Clue Crew. Or turn the page to find out who dunnit!

1. Nancy believes the chewed-up purple Pogo bracelet was Wesley's. Why would Wesley want to leave Pogo in the goat yoga class? Write down some reasons on a piece of paper.

2. The Clue Crew ruled out all of their suspects. Can you think of any others? Write them down on a piece of paper.

3. Pogo ran amok through the whole goat yoga class! Why do you think the little goat went wild? Write your reasons on a piece of paper.

Chapter

GO, POGO, GO!

Nancy brought Chip home. Then she hurried with Bess and George to Wesley's house.

George still had her soccer ball. She kicked it all the way to Magnolia Street.

"Let's go straight to the backyard," Nancy said as they approached the Disher house. "That's where Wesley usually is when he's spending time with Pogo."

The Clue Crew rounded the house to the backyard. The trampoline was still set up, but there was no sign of anyone, not even Pogo.

Bess pointed to a small green-colored shed in the far corner of the yard. "Why doesn't that little house have a door?" she asked.

"It could be a run-in shed," George said. "You know, like a doghouse."

"Or a goat house," Nancy said with a smile. "Let's check it out."

George playfully tossed the ball into Bess's arms. While she and Nancy entered the shed, Bess stayed outside, bouncing the ball on the grass.

"It's kind of dark in here," Nancy said, looking around the shed, "but I see bags of goat chow, grooming brushes, water dishes, and lots of hay."

George turned to the wall and grinned. "I see just what we're looking for."

"What?" Nancy asked.

"*Boom!*" George said as she pulled a long belt-like object off a hook. "One green leash with white polka dots!"

"George!" Nancy gasped. "You found it!"

"Um . . . you guys," Bess called from outside. "I found something too."

"What, Bess?" Nancy asked as she and George exited the goat shed.

Not saying a word, Bess pointed to the roof. Nancy and George glanced up. Staring down at them from the top of the shed was Pogo!

"Baaaaaaa!"

Pogo backed up, then took a running leap off the roof, landing on all fours!

Startled, Bess let go of the ball, shooting it into the air. Pogo bleated as he jumped up to butt the ball hard with his head. The soccer ball arched way over the yard, right toward Wesley!

"Whoa!" he cried as he ducked. The ball soared over his head. "I never saw Pogo do that before."

Wesley chased the ball down, picked it up, and carried it back to Nancy, Bess, and George. "What are you guys doing here?" he asked. "You didn't come to play soccer, did you?"

Nancy was ready to explain everything. She took a deep breath, then said, "You already know that someone snuck Pogo into the Sweet Creams Farm goat pen yesterday. He ruined the whole yoga class."

"Did you bring Pogo to the farm, Wesley?" Bess asked.

Wesley stared at the girls, then let the ball drop to the ground. "What makes you think I did it?" he asked.

George had been holding Pogo's leash behind her back. She held it up for Wesley to see. "This matches the green collar Pogo was wearing yesterday," she said.

"So?" Wesley asked.

"So, there's more," Bess said. "Show him the bracelet, Nancy."

Nancy held up the purple Pogo bracelet. "We found this stuck on the goat pen gate yesterday. It has tiny teeth marks on it."

"As if a little goat chewed it," George added. She nodded at Wesley's wrist. "By the way, where's your Pogo bracelet?"

Wesley tried pulling his sleeve down over his

wrist. Blushing, he shifted his weight from side to side. "Okay, I did bring Pogo to the farm yesterday. But not to ruin your yoga class!"

"Then why did you bring him?" Nancy asked.

"Pogo was getting in trouble here for chewing stuff up—mostly Leslie's things," Wesley explained. "The book I have on raising a pet goat has a whole chapter on what goats need to make them happy."

"What do they need?" Bess asked.

"Other goats," Wesley replied. "The book says, 'An only goat is a lonely goat.'"

"Is that why you brought Pogo to the farm yesterday?" Nancy asked. "To make friends?"

"I guess." Wesley sighed.

"Why didn't you just ask Sophie if you could put Pogo in the pen?" George asked. "And why didn't you stick around to watch him?"

"I was afraid Sophie would say no, so I secretly left Pogo in the pen with the other goats and came straight home." Wesley's shoulders drooped. "I had no idea Pogo went bonkers in the yoga class until the guy from Sweet Creams brought him home."

Nancy couldn't help feeling bad for Wesley. He hadn't meant to do anything wrong. He just wanted Pogo to be happy.

"Pogo probably did like being with the other goats," Nancy said, smiling. "He just didn't like yoga that much."

"Baaaaa!" Pogo bleated.

Everyone looked at Pogo. The little goat was prancing through the yard, kicking the soccer ball over and over with his tiny hoof!

"Hey," George exclaimed as she watched her ball roll across the grass. "That's it!"

"What's it?" Nancy asked.

"Pogo may not like yoga," George said with a grin, "but I bet he'll like something else!"

"Go, Pogo, go!" Nancy cheered as Wesley's goat sprinted after the rolling ball. But this time he wasn't alone. Pogo was running with the other Pygmy goats from Sweet Creams Farm!

Racing alongside the goats that morning were Nancy, Bess, George, and their friends.

The crew from *Wake Up, River Heights* was there too. But this time they hadn't come to report on a goat yoga class. They were there to film *goat soccer*!

"What says spring to kids more than soccer?" Stephanie Burns said to the camera. "Today at Sweet Creams Farm, some of those kids are goats!"

"Baaaaa!" Pogo bleated as he scampered past Nancy, Bess, and George. Wesley caught up with them, all smiles.

"Pogo is totally loving soccer with his new

friends!" Wesley said, "and Sophie says I can bring him to the farm whenever I want!"

As Wesley ran to catch up with Pogo, Bess turned to Nancy and George. "I'm happy the Clue Crew solved another case," she said. "And I'm even happier that Pogo is happy."

"Me too," Nancy said. "I guess Pogo is more into soccer than yoga after all."

"Hey, whatever floats your boat," George said before kicking the ball in Pogo's direction. "Or should we say, *goat*?"

Test your detective skills with even more Clue Book mysteries:

Nancy Drew Clue Book #16: Duck Derby Debacle

"Hundreds of rubber duckies!" Bess Marvin exclaimed. "Can you imagine so many in one place?"

"Or in one bathtub?" George Fayne joked.

Nancy giggled as she and her two best friends walked together, enjoying the summer afternoon. That Friday, the air was as warm as cookies fresh from the oven. It was also full of excitement!

"There'll be lots of room for all those rubber ducks when they race down the river on Sunday," Nancy said. "And we'll be there to watch!"

The girls couldn't wait until Sunday, but it was

already fun-day. There was pre-derby festival at Mayor Strong's house that afternoon, and it was just for kids!

"How will anyone know whose rubber duck wins the race?" Bess asked. "Most rubber duckies look alike."

"Each rubber duck will have a number, Bess," Nancy explained. "The first to float past the finish line wins."

George gave a thumbs-up as she said, "The owner of the winning duck wins a summer of free movies at the cineplex—popcorn included!"

"Then I'm glad our families have ducks in the race," Bess said. "I just wish kids were allowed to enter too."

"Me too," George said. "Then we'd really be a part of the rubber ducky derby."

Nancy wished they could be more involved as well. There had to be more for them to do than cheer for the racing ducks. Suddenly she had an idea.

"Maybe we can help out at the ducky derby!"

"Help out how?" Bess asked.

"Let's ask Mayor Strong when we get to his house," Nancy said with a smile. "There must be something we can do to be a big part of the ducky derby!"

The celebration had already begun when Nancy, Bess, and George arrived at the mayor's mansion. There were tables filled with duck-yellow cupcakes and duck-shaped cookies. There were games, too, like a rubber duck toss. Most of the kids were standing in front of a stage, waiting to watch the River Heights Junior Dancers rock out a number called "Disco Duck."

Nancy, Bess, and George were about to join the crowd when a voice shouted, "There's still time to buy a rubber duck for the derby, plus a chance to win the big prize!"

The voice came from a table set up near the gate. Behind it, a man and two women were selling rubber ducks for five dollars apiece. When they made a sale, the volunteer would toss a duck into a cardboard box. Nancy giggled as each landed with a squeak. The ducks sounded like her puppy Chocolate Chip's squeaky chew toys!

"Remember, everybody!" a woman selling ducks called out. "The money raised will be used to build benches around the River Heights Park duck pond!"

"How many ducks do you think they've sold so far?" Bess asked.

Nancy was about to guess when a voice behind them said, "As of five minutes ago—two hundred eighty ducks."

The girls turned to see Kinsley Armbruster from one of the other third grade classes at school. She wore a bright yellow cap with an orange duck bill and dangly ducky earrings.

"Two hundred eighty ducks, huh?" George said, scrunching her face thoughtfully. "At five dollars apiece . . . that equals one thousand four hundred dollars."

"George won the math bee last week," Nancy said proudly.

"Wow," Kinsley said, clearly impressed. "And I thought the Clue Crew just solved mysteries!"

Nancy, Bess, and George did love solving

mysteries—so much so that they called themselves the Clue Crew. They even had a clue book where they wrote down all their clues and suspects.

"Don't you collect rubber duckies, Kinsley?" Nancy asked.

"Yes," Kinsley said, gazing at the table. "But I only have a hundred rubber duckies. I wish I had more."

"More?" George asked. "Aren't a hundred rubber duckies enough?"

"Not if I want to break the record." Kinsley replied.

"What record?" Bess asked.

"The Kids' World Book of Records," Kinsley said. "I just need a couple hundred more ducks to break the rubber ducky collection record. Then they'd post my name on their website and I'd be famous!"

"There's still time to collect more," Nancy said.

"Not really," Kinsley sighed. "A judge from the Kids' World Book of Records is coming to my house this afternoon to count my ducks."

Bess glanced at her watch. "It's already one thirty. Shouldn't you be home getting ready for the judge's visit?"

Kinsley's duck earrings wiggled as she shook her head. "I want to stay here until three o'clock. They're giving out free T-shirts at the end of the celebration!"

Kinsley gave the girls a little wave, then headed toward the stage to watch the dancers.

"Kinsley loves collecting duck stuff," Bess said. "Maybe I should start collecting something too."

"You already have a huge collection, Bess," George said.

"Of what?" Bess asked.

George looked Bess up and down and said, "Clothes! The judge of the *Kids' World Book of Records* should check out your closet!"

Bess rolled her eyes. She and George were cousins, but they were totally different. Bess had long blond hair and the latest fashion-forward clothes and accessories. Dark-haired George loved clothes too, as long as they were comfy enough to do cartwheels in. She was also an electronics geek—and proud of it!

"There's Mayor Strong," Nancy said with a smile. "Let's ask him about helping out at the ducky derby!"

Mayor Strong turned when he heard Nancy, Bess, and George call his name, beaming as he recognized the city's best young sleuths. "What can I do for you girls?" he asked.

Just as Nancy opened her mouth to reply, a woman stepped between her and the mayor. The girls recognized her at once. It was Dorothy Danner, River Heights's busiest party planner. The Clue Crew knew Dorothy from a missing butterfly case they once worked on. They also knew she could be a drama queen!

"Excuse me, Mayor Strong," Dorothy said briskly. "I need to talk to you at once."

"I was just speaking with the girls, Dorothy," Mayor Strong said. "Can it wait a minute?"

"Not even a second!" Dorothy declared. "This is an emergency!"

Nancy, Bess, and George traded glances. Everything with Dorothy was an emergency.

"I'm planning a baby shower tomorrow morning for Eileen MacDuff," Dorothy explained. "The theme is rubber duckies."

"Mrs. MacDuff?" Nancy asked grinning. "She's our school librarian."

"Mrs. MacDuff picks out the best books for us to read!" Bess said.

"And she doesn't make us whisper in her library," George added.

Dorothy raised an eyebrow at the girls. "How nice," she said, not smiling, then turned back to the mayor. "Mayor Strong, I'm going to need about a hundred rubber ducks to decorate the table."

"So what's the problem?" Mayor Strong asked.

"My order went to the wrong address," Dorothy wailed. "It's too late to have them redelivered!" She shook her head. "Every store in River Heights donated their ducks to this silly ducky derby!"

Nancy, Bess, and George stared at Dorothy. How could she call the ducky derby silly?

"How can I help, Dorothy?" Mayor Strong asked.

Dorothy pointed to the table just as one of the volunteers dropped another duck into the box. "Let me buy those rubber duckies for the baby shower."

Mayor Strong shook his head. "Sorry, Dorothy. Those ducks have already been sold. They're racing in the derby on Sunday."

"All of them?" Dorothy cried.

The mayor nodded and said, "I'm afraid you'll have to cook up something else."

Dorothy stared at the mayor for a moment, and then her expression shifted. "Cook up something, huh?" she murmured. "Now, there's an idea."

A suddenly excited Dorothy brushed past the girls. She didn't notice bumping George's shoulder as she rushed off.

"Sounds like Dorothy's planning something," Nancy said.

George crossed her arms. "She *is* a party planner, just like my mom, remember?"

"How could we forget?" Bess asked, licking her lips. "Aunt Louise saves us the yummiest leftovers from her parties!"

Mayor Strong glanced toward the stage. "Can your question wait, girls? I have to start up the duck joke contest."

"Sure, Mayor Strong," Nancy said.

George's eyes flashed as the mayor walked away. "Duck joke contest? I know the most awesome duck joke!"

"Tell us, George!" Nancy pleaded.

Bess giggled. "Yes, George! Quack us up!"

"Okay," George said with a grin. "What do you get when you fill a box with ducks?"

Before Nancy and Bess could guess, George blurted out, "A box of quackers! Get it?"

"I got it!" an angry voice snapped. "And I want to get it *back*!"

Nancy Drew
✴ CLUE BOOK ✴

Test your detective skills with Nancy and her best friends, Bess and George!

NancyDrew.com

EBOOK EDITIONS ALSO AVAILABLE
From Aladdin ✴ simonandschuster.com/kids

READ & LEARN
with
simon kids

Keep your child reading, learning, and having fun with Simon Kids!

A one-stop shop where you can
**find downloadable resources, watch interactive autho
videos, browse books by reading level, and more!**

Visit us at
SimonandSchusterPublishing.com/ReadandLearn/

And follow us @SimonKids

SIMON & SCHUSTER
Children's Publishing

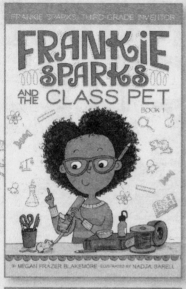

FOLLOW THE TRAIL AND SOLVE
MYSTERIES WITH FRANK AND JOE!

HardyBoysSeries.com

Don't miss the Mindy Kim series!

ALADDIN | SIMON & SCHUSTER, NEW YORK

EBOOK EDITIONS ALSO AVAILABLE